Pedrito's Day

LUIS GARAY

Orchard Books · New York

Copyright © 1997 by Luis Garay

First American Edition 1997 published by Orchard Books

First published in Canada
by Stoddart Publishing Co. Limited in 1997

Orchard Books
95 Madison Avenue
New York, NY 10016

Library of Congress Cataloging-in-Publication Data

Garay, Luis.

Pedrito's day / Luis Garay. – 1st American ed.
p. cm.

Summary: When Pedrito replaces, from his own earnings,
money he has lost, his mother decides that he is finally
big enough for some of his father's earnings
to be used towards buying him a bicycle.

ISBN 0-531-09522-3

[1. Latin Americans–Fiction.   2. Responsibility–Fiction.]
I. Title.

PZ7.G15435Pe 1997 96-28392

Printed in Hong Kong

10   9   8   7   6   5   4   3   2   1

To the memory of Violeta Arguello
and to
Kathy Lowinger for all of her support

There was a Pedro, but he had gone North to work. So now there was only Pedrito — little Pedro — at home with his mama and his *abuela*. Every month they waited anxiously for news from his papa, Pedro. In every letter Pedro would ask, "Is he big enough yet?"

Pedrito knew the reason for the question — when he grew big enough, some of the money Pedro sent home would be added to Pedrito's own earnings and used to buy him what he wanted most: a bicycle. He and Mama could carry their market loads on it. He could ride it over the bumpy lane as if the bicycle were a stallion. But best of all, owning a bicycle would mean that he was big, almost as big as Pedro himself.

Though it was early when Mama and Pedrito rose to work in the market, the sun was already cutting through the cracks of the shutters, and the *flap flap* of Abuela's hands as she shaped tortillas rang from the patio.

Every day Mama sold Abuela's tortillas and tamales, and Pedrito shined shoes. Pedrito did not mind the work, because each day brought him closer to his dream, to a bicycle painted sky blue with firm wheels and a tan leather seat and a straw basket for carrying things. Every day he stashed some of the coins he earned in a little purse he kept inside his shoe-shine kit. The purse was growing heavier.

Soon the tortillas were a golden heap in the basket. Mama hoisted the basket to her head. Pedrito followed her down the dusty lane. "Our loads would be lighter if we had a bicycle, Mama."

She had heard this before. "Someday, Pedrito."

Pedrito smiled as he thought of Mama's surprise when he could show her his purse full of coins.

By the time they reached the market, it seemed to shimmer in the hot morning sun. The heavy smell of fruit and roasting corn lay in the air. Flies buzzed and dogs barked. Tía Paula called a welcome from her fruit stand.

"May I go now, Mama?" Pedrito was anxious to take his place among the boys shining shoes close by. The early morning was his busiest time. The men who worked in the big offices wanted their shoes to shine like mirrors.

"Help me first, *chiquito*," said his mother. Pedrito helped Mama place a heavy plank over a wooden crate and arrange the tamales and tortillas just so.

Pedrito opened his shoe-shine kit. A pair of linen-clad legs approached. Pedrito did his job so well that the shoes gleamed. Three coins clunked into his shoe-shine box. He stowed them carefully in his purse. But before he could shake out his cloth in preparation for his next customer, Tía Paula called out to Pedrito.

"Pedrito, *chiquito*, I want you to run an errand." Oh no! If he left his spot, he would miss the customers who might pass by. "Fetch me change from Tía Blanca." Pedrito closed his kit, his lips thin with impatience. He stuffed the bill Tía Paula handed him into his pocket and went to find Tía Blanca in the lane where the newly made hats and baskets smelled like a freshly mown meadow.

He ran by the boys who were playing soccer in the street along the market. "Come and join us, Pedrito," they called. "We can't make up even sides." The older boys had never asked him to play before. Thrilled, Pedrito joined their game. The boys kicked the ball, raising clouds of dust over their heads. They all knew they should be working, but the ball swept back and forth, drawing them in as if it were weaving a spell.

Although neither side had won, the summer heat ended the game. Pedrito felt more grown-up than he ever had as he sat with the older boys on the curb. Then, with a terrible start, he remembered — Tía Paula! Frantically he looked in his pockets. The money was gone!

He searched the street, but the bill had disappeared, a scrap of paper scudding in the wind. Somebody surely would have picked it up by now. The money was lost forever.

Pedrito was miserable. He thought about what to do. Perhaps he could tell Tía Paula that a robber in a mask had taken the money and that all this time he had been helping the police catch the thief. Or perhaps he could say that a bird had swooped down and grabbed it from his hand. Or perhaps he could just run far away.

But Pedrito knew what he should do. His stomach clenched tight and his feet heavy, he made his way back to Tía Paula's stand. He took a deep breath. "I lost the money," Pedrito said. Tía Paula's face turned red. She looked like she would burst with angry words.

Pedrito stopped her. "I am going to replace it," he said. He pulled out the purse of coins he had hidden in his kit. He counted out the coins he needed. The purse felt much lighter. Almost half of his bicycle money was gone.

Dismally he set up his stand again, but no customers stopped in the afternoon heat.

Finally the long afternoon passed. Pedrito and Mama walked home. There were no tamales or tortillas in Mama's basket, but she carried corn flour she had bought and a length of cloth for a new shirt. "Your shirt is too small, Pedrito," she explained. "I will have to sew for you again." She paused. "Tía Paula told me what happened."

"I was a baby," said Pedrito. "I lost the money."

"Yes, but you were also brave. You admitted it, and you replaced the money."

A pool of light from the window welcomed them home. Pedrito longed for his *abuela*'s voice as they stepped into their tiny patio. She greeted them eagerly, a letter in her hand. Pedro had sent it from the North. Folded with the thin paper was money. "We will pay the rent first, and then we will . . ."

". . . then we will put some aside for a bicycle for Pedrito," finished Mama. "Now he is big enough."